For Gabriel, who gives the best hugs —J. M.

For Maxwell & Yvonne —S. H.

Text copyright © 2008 by James Mayhew
Illustrations copyright © 2008 by Sue Hellard
All rights reserved. No part of this book may be used or reproduced
in any manner whatsoever without written permission from the publisher,
except in the case of brief quotations embodied in critical articles or reviews.

Typeset in Garamond MT
Art created with watercolor

First published in Great Britain in 2008 by Bloomsbury Publishing Plc.
Published in the United States in 2008 by Bloomsbury U.S.A. Children's Books
175 Fifth Avenue, New York, NY 10010
Distributed to the trade by Holtzbrinck Publishers

Library of Congress Cataloging-in-Publication Data
Mayhew, James.
Where's my hug? / by James Mayhew ; illustrations by Sue Hellard. — 1st U.S. ed.
p.   cm.
Summary: Jake tries to track down his mother's hug after she gives it to his father,
who gives it to the cat, who gives it to a witch, and so on.
ISBN-13: 978-1-59990-225-8 • ISBN-10: 1-59990-225-7 (hardcover)
[1. Hugging—Fiction. 2. Mothers and sons—Fiction.] I. Hellard, Susan, ill. II. Title.
III. Title: Where is my hug?
PZ7.M4684Wh 2008   [E]—dc22   2007026306

First U.S. Edition 2008
Printed in China
3 5 7 9 10 8 6 4

© Mixed Sources
Product group from well-managed
forests, controlled sources and
recycled wood or fibre
FSC   www.fsc.org Cert no. SCS-COC-00927
© 1996 Forest Stewardship Council

Where's My Hug?

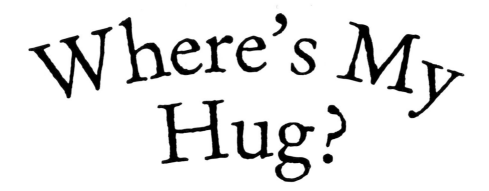

James Mayhew

illustrated by Sue Hellard

BLOOMSBURY
CHILDREN'S
BOOKS

Jake said good-bye at the school door.

"Come give me a hug," said Mom.

"MOM!" said Jake. "I don't want a hug.
Everyone will think I'm a baby."

And Jake ran off to play.

But at the end of the day, things hadn't gone
Jake's way. So he asked his mom,

"Where's my hug?"

"You said you didn't want it,
so I gave it to Dad," said Mom.

So Jake said to Dad,

"Where's my hug?"

"I gave it to the cat," said Dad.

Jake went to the cat.

"Where's my hug?"

he asked.

"I gave it to a witch," she said,
"because she gave me a tasty fish."

Jake went to the witch and asked,

"Where's my hug?"

"I gave it to a wizard," said the witch,
"because his spell went wrong."

So Jake went to the wizard.

"Where's my hug?"

he asked.

"Goodness!" said the wizard.
"I gave it to a knight in armor
who was off to see a dragon."

Jake found the knight.

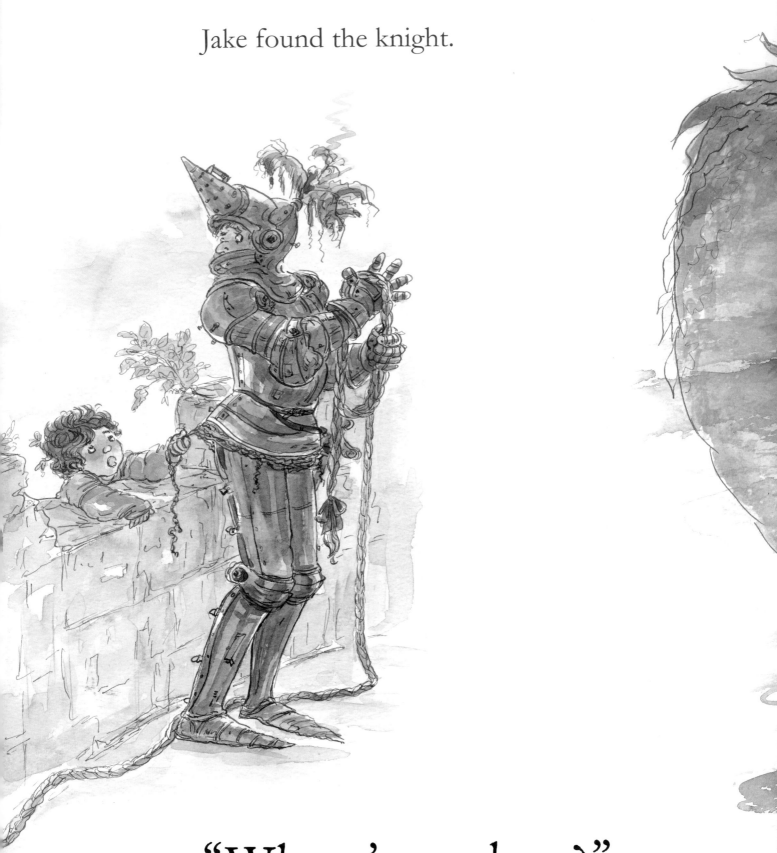

"Where's my hug?"

asked Jake.

"I gave it to
the princess,"
said the knight.

Jake went over to the princess.

"Where's my hug?"

"It was a good hug, and it made me brave,"
said the princess, "so I gave it to the dragon
and tamed him with it."

Jake said to the dragon,

"Give me
my hug!"

"That's no way to ask," said the dragon.

"Can I have my hug, PLEASE?" asked Jake.

And the dragon
gave him a hug.

Jake rode home with the knight and the princess
and the dragon, just in time for dinner.

And after dinner, Mom put him to bed and said,
"Now can I have MY hug, please?"

"Well," said Jake, "I want to keep it!"

"What if I give you another one?" said Mom,
hugging Jake.

"Then I'll give you this one," said Jake.
"But be careful who you give it to."